CINNAMON KISSES AND GINGERBREAD WISHES

Kathleen Ryder

DEDICATION

For everyone who believes in the
magic of Christmas.

CHAPTER ONE

Holly looked around her and sighed. Christmas was her favourite time of the year; her mother had named her aptly. Holly loved everything about Christmas, from the never-ending carols that played from every speaker to the Christmas, treats she could finally enjoy guilt-free, from the scores of handwritten Christmas cards that she sent each year, to the happy couples all around, holding hands and laughing, kissing and making plans. Holly loved the romance of Christmas, loved the hope and the excitement, the joy and the discovery. To Holly, it seemed as if romance itself was magnified at Christmastime, that it was somehow larger than life, that little bit more special than the everyday romance that occurred on any other normal day throughout the year. Not that Holly would know personally, not having anything to compare it to.

At almost thirty-eight years old, Holly had never had a serious relationship. In fact, her last relationship only lasted three dates, before Holly admitted what she had known all along, that they were not at all suited. Her best friend and neighbour, Finn, had tried to tell her so, but Holly had refused to listen, only admitting later that he had been right all along. Holly sighed again, tomorrow was the start of December, and usually, she would have been giddy with excitement, but not this year. Lately, Holly had been feeling restless, unsettled, and, although she hated to admit it, even to herself, more than a little bit jealous of all of the couples that seemed to surround her.

Holly knew why of course; she was tired of being alone. She was tired of being the only single person in her group of friends, the spare wheel, the odd one out. Well, not quite the only one, Finn was also single. Holly smiled at the thought of her best friend. They had been inseparable since they first met, Holly had been nine years old, and had just been sent to live with her grandmother. Suffering from a trauma-induced muteness, the result of being the only surviving passenger in the car crash that had killed both of her parents, it had been Finn's constant presence, both in Holly's life and in Holly's grandmother's apple tree, that had finally brought her out of her world of silence. Holly's longest relationship ever was with Finn, a fact that was not lost on her. The simple fact was, Holly was in a rut. As much as she loved having Sunday lunch with Finn and his family, and looked forward to Friday nights curled up on her couch with Finn, a great movie, and some snacks, it wasn't helping her find Mr Perfect. It wasn't as if he was going to suddenly drop through her ceiling and onto her lap, no, if Holly wanted to find Mr Perfect, she knew that she was going to have to go out and find him herself.

Which is why she found herself sitting in the middle of the Esplanade, on market day, surrounded by hordes of tourists looking to snare an early Christmas bargain.

"Holly!" Holly looked around, she would recognise that voice anywhere, as familiar to her as her own. There, a few tables away, was Finn, waving at her, as he attempted to weave his way through the pedestrians to get to her. "Urgh! Sorry, I'm late." He flopped himself into the chair next to Holly, kissing her on her cheek as he did. "The traffic was chaos! I literally had to park three blocks away and walk." He shuddered, shaking his head at the craziness while Holly tried not to laugh at his obvious distaste for crowds and people. Finn was very much a homebody.

While he had left home and gone to study at a prestigious pastry school, he had been all too happy to return, and stay, buying the property across the road from his parent's house when it had been placed on the market. Holly had asked Finn once if the reason he lived so close to his parents was because of his Greek heritage, and he had told her that it was because he loved them. Unashamedly honest, one of the reasons Holly cherished her friendship with Finn so much. She quite literally could not imagine her life without him in it.

"So, not that I wouldn't go anywhere with you, no questions asked," Finn started, "but why exactly are we here?" Finn picked up the menu from the table stand and started to flip through it.

"We are here," Holly lowered the menu to look him in the eyes, hitting him with her most winning smile, "so that you can help me to find my Mr Perfect." The menu hit the table with a thud, Finn's jaw went slack, his mouth hung open. There was nothing but silence. Finn stared at Holly, he blinked, once, twice.

"You can't be serious. You want me to help you find your Mr Perfect?" He sounded incredulous. "How on earth could I possibly help you do that?"

"Finn," Holly cajoled, "you know me better than anyone else, I trust you explicitly. Besides," she added as an afterthought, "I have a plan."

"You have a plan?"

"Uh-huh." Holly's eyes sparkled with mischief. Finn groaned.

"Holly is this going to be like the time you had a plan to modernise the bakery, and nearly ended up flooding the entire building? Or will it be more like the time you decided to use foraged herbs and nettles to update your grandmother's spiced pear cake and gave us all food poisoning?" Finn had every right to be wary, Holly didn't have the best track record with executing what seemed like fantastic ideas at the time.

"Haha, very funny," Holly muttered. "This time my plan is crazy, which is why it will work."

"Okay, I'm listening."

"I plan to find Mr Perfect before Christmas, actually, I am going to give myself seven days in which to find him."

"Seven days?! Are you crazy?"

"Most likely Finn, but this is the deadline. People fall in love all of the time; some people claim to fall in love at first sight. I'm giving it seven days. If I haven't found Mr Perfect by then, well, I will stop looking and resign myself to a life of singledom." Holly shrugged matter of factly. She had given this a lot of thought, well, she had thought about it as she drifted off to sleep last night, and at the time it had seemed like a great plan, inspired actually. When she woke this morning, it had still seemed like a good idea, albeit a little daft and slightly unachievable, but regardless, Holly was willing to give it a shot. After all, it wasn't as if she had anything to lose, in fact, she had everything to gain. "So, will you help me, Finn?"

"I think it is insane Holly, I really do, you can't possibly find Mr Perfect in seven days, it isn't realistic, and I don't want you getting hurt if this plan isn't successful. That said, it does sound like rather a fantastic adventure, so yes, I will help you."

CHAPTER TWO

Finn listened in fascination as Holly outlined her seven-day plan for finding Mr Perfect. He tried not to stare at her lips as she spoke, he really did, but they were captivating. A perfect cupid's bow, turned up slightly at the corners in her ever-ready smile, shiny and glossy, coated in her signature ballet slipper pink lip gloss. They were mesmerising, and ever so kissable, not that he would know, of course, never having found the courage to actually tell Holly that he was in love with her and that he had been in love with her for the past several years. Finn sighed softly, he wondered if he would ever find the courage to tell Holly exactly how he felt about her. There was a reason that Finn was still single, he had already found his perfect mate, his soul mate, his one true love. He was just too shy to tell her. She was his best friend, his confidant, and the fear, the possibility, that he could ruin it all by confessing his true feelings to her, was enough to paralyse him into silence.

To be honest, Finn was surprised that Holly didn't know that he was in love with her, he had never been especially good with keeping secrets, and as hard as he had tried to keep his feelings hidden, he knew that there were some people who had already guessed exactly how he felt about Holly. Holly's grandmother had known, she had summoned Finn across the road to visit with her, shortly before her death earlier in the year. She hadn't beaten around the bush, instead, getting straight to the point, telling Finn that she knew that he was in love with her granddaughter, and asking him exactly what he had intended to do about the situation. She had not been at all impressed when Finn had confessed to her that he had no intention of risking his friendship with Holly, and in fact, was planning on keeping his feelings for her a secret. Not one to pull punches, Holly's grandmother had told Finn that he was a fool and that she knew that he and Holly belonged together, he just had to believe it himself.

Finn could remember the exact moment that he knew that he was in love with Holly. Several years ago, they had attended a mutual friends hen night, which had been held at a rather unusual boutique venue, reminiscent of something out of a vintage circus, or perhaps some type of retro gentlemen's club. The decor had been insane, full-length crazy mirrors, merry go round horses scattered throughout, and board games underneath the glass tabletops. There were chandeliers made from various parts of old dolls, vintage circus posters adorned the walls, and at the entrance, and a life-sized statue of a lion. The venue room that they had used was set up with karaoke, carnival games, and in prime position, a stripper's pole.

After one too many glasses of champagne, Holly had climbed up onto the stage, mounting the stripper's pole like a paid performer. The combination of Holly's blood-red stilettos, the fabric of her dress riding dangerously high on her thighs, and the way her mouth pouted ever so slightly as she danced with the pole, left Finn unable to breathe. It was in that instant that he knew that he was in love with her, knew that he wanted her, knew that nobody else should ever have her. As much as it destroyed him to see her go on a date with another man, he kept quiet. He sat back and smiled and pretended that it wasn't killing him inside to see Holly date a string of men, all of whom were all wrong for her. He would not risk losing their friendship, not for anything. And now he was too late. If he told her now, if he confessed to Holly his true feelings, she wouldn't believe him, she would think that he was trying to talk her out of her plan.

A plan that he had just agreed to help her with, a plan that, if it worked, would mean he would never be able to tell Holly the truth about his feelings for her, which meant that he had seven days. Seven days in which to convince Holly that he is the one, that he is her Mr Perfect. Mr Perfect For Always, not just Mr Perfect For Now. He just needed his own plan.

"How will you know when you have found your Mr Perfect Holly?"

"Oh, that's easy," she dismissed his concerns with a wave of her hand, "I have a list."

"A list?" He smiled across at her indulgently, it was just like Holly to have a list for this, she was the queen of lists, she even had a list of lists to make.

"Well, more like criteria I guess."

"Tell me?"

"Okay." She nodded, fishing around in her oversized handbag until she had found what she had been looking for, triumphantly holding aloft a sheet of paper.

"Okay," she started, "I have nine criteria. One," she read it off her list, "and it should go without saying, he has to be family orientated. I'm not interested in anyone who thinks that spending time with his family is a chore instead of a pleasure. Two, I want someone who is thoughtful and considerate towards myself and to others. Three, he needs to be hardworking, and he has to enjoy whatever career he is in. Four, he needs to know his own mind. I want someone who I can have a real conversation with, about the things that matter. I want someone who I can argue with from time to time, not someone who is always in complete agreeance with me. Five, I want someone who is community-minded, someone who is happy to help those that are less fortunate than himself, someone who treats everyone as equal, regardless of whether they wash his car or belong to his golf club. Six, I'm not interested in sports." Holly grimaced. "Ideally he won't be either. I'd love it if he shared my passions, watching movies, trash and treasure markets, pottering about at home. Simple is joyful for me, I would hope it would be for him as well." She paused to take a sip of her bottle of water.

"Seven, he needs to be able to make me laugh, that's a deal-breaker. Eight, I'm not interested in anyone who is sexist or who thinks that it is his job to mow the lawn while I cook his dinner. I want someone who is an equal partner. Nine, he must want to have children, because that is something that I want. Two, maybe three. Huh, that's interesting." Holly grew silent, suddenly very interested in memorising the list in her hands.

"Is that it?" Finn prompted.

"Hmm?" Holly looked up, distracted. "Oh, yes. Well, I mean, looks aren't important to me, as long as he is kind.

Oh, and honest, obviously. I am not interested in dating a liar, no matter how many other criteria he meets on my list."

"No," Finn grew cold despite sitting in the glorious sunshine, "of course not."

CHAPTER THREE

Opening her front door, Holly paused, turning on the spot and looking across the road at Finn, also at his front door. She waved a final goodbye before walking inside and closing her door. Holly was feeling all keyed up, having told Finn all about her plan for finding Mr Perfect within seven days, Holly was excited to get started. Although he had been initially reluctant, Finn had turned out to be a wonderful resource, after going through Holly's list of requirements, or criteria as she had called them, he had been full of ideas of where she could meet somebody who would match, based on paper in any case. One could never really plan for chemistry. Holly had been slightly surprised that Finn had not protested more, secretly she had hoped that he would. They had been best friends for years, it was silly to think that that dynamic would change now, wasn't it?

They were going to start implementing their plan tomorrow, and Holly was surprised to realise that she was actually nervous. She wasn't sure why, after all, it had been her idea in the first place, to step out of her comfort zone, to try something that she would not normally do. Finn had helped Holly to zone in on potential places where she could potentially meet her Mr Perfect. They had decided to try a different place each day, after all, Holly and Finn still had to go to work, they couldn't spend all day trawling around town looking for Holly's Mr Perfect. Tomorrow they were going to go to the grocery store, Finn seemed convinced that it was a fantastic place to go to pick up a date. Holly wasn't quite as convinced, never having tried it before, but Finn was adamant, she needed to go to the produce section of the grocery store and look at buying some stone fruit.

Holly wasn't sure if he was being totally serious, but she would find out tomorrow.

In the meantime, Holly was far too wound up to be able to settle down and relax. Her future was full of possibilities, a fact that both excited and scared her. Holly had intended on spending the afternoon sitting down and getting some accounts written up, but she knew that there was no way that she would be able to concentrate on such a menial task. It was the one aspect of owning a business that truly bored her, the paperwork. Unfortunately for Holly, it was also the most vital aspect of owning her own business, and one that she was unable to afford to pay anybody else to do at this stage. When Holly had first opened her own bakery, she had been fresh out of university, having studied a degree in business. Holly had dreamed of owning her own bakery since she was a little girl, it was a dream come true, combining her natural flair for baking with her business degree, and Finn's skills as a pastry chef. Although One More Bite had been operating for almost ten years now, it was still a small family affair. Apart from Finn, Holly also employed Finn's teenage nephew part-time, to work the counter on their busy weekends, and Finn's dad was her delivery driver.

Maybe one day Holly would expand, but for now, she enjoyed the creativity and uniqueness of being a boutique bakery. Hers was the only bakery of its kind, blending the ancient with the modern. Holly loved taking her great-great grandmother's recipes and substituting the listed ingredients for something that was foraged or unusual instead. It gave Holly a sense of ownership, of creativity, to be able to alter and concoct something new from a recipe that a distant relative had once created and used every day. Holly had a room full of recipe books, none of the women in her family had ever thrown any of them out. The collection was hers now, a timeline of her family, stories woven throughout the generations, handwritten notes in the margins, little tips and hints, mixed with the occasional anecdote and observation.

Holly would often find herself in this room, the recipe vault as it had always been called. Holly had no idea what it was before it became the recipe vault, much like the recipe books, this house had also been in her family for generations, Holly having inherited it from her grandmother, and her grandmother having inherited it from her mother before her and so on throughout history. The room had always had a calming effect on Holly, and it was this room where she now found herself, curling up on the window seat at the bay window, overlooking her grandmother's rose garden. Holly idly picked up a book of the stack closet to her, flipping through the pages, pausing at one covered in scrawled handwriting. The traced the name of the recipe with her fingertip. Holly Cakes. Unusual, and not one that Holly remembered seeing before. She skimmed the ingredients list, smiling as she realised that she had all of the ingredients on hand.

Holly hummed to herself as she padded through to the kitchen, opening and closing cabinet doors, ferreting around until she found the ingredients that she needed, gathering them all up on the kitchen bench. She turned her stereo on, blasting Christmas carols throughout her otherwise quiet house. Holly perched on the kitchen stool; the recipe book opened in front of her. As she read through the recipe, a frown appeared on her face. She shook her head and started reading again.

"What the?" She muttered to herself. "This can't be right." Holly started reading again, from the top, slowly, so as not to misinterpret anything. The recipe read as if it were a spell. Thumbing through the rest of the recipe book, Holly could see that all of the recipes it contained sounded as if they were from a spellbook. Holly closed the book and pushed it away, mentally arguing with herself.

They couldn't really be spells, could they? After all, her grandmother wasn't a witch, not by a long shot. As far as she knew, there were no ancestors who were even rumoured to be eccentric enough to be classified as a witch. Not that Holly believed in witches anyway, not really. She believed that there were things that were not easy to explain, and she believed in the spirit of magic, much like the spirit of Christmas, of hope and of belief and of love. She did not believe in cackling old hags hunched over a large bubbling black cauldrons full of hissing and spitting green liquid, muttering and chanting like some sort of cartoon caricature. Still, Holly picked up the recipe book again, it couldn't hurt to make these cakes, could it? If she didn't believe in spells then saying the words as she baked wouldn't cause any harm, would it? Deciding that she was right, that casting a spell was rather a lot like believing in superstitions, they only worked if you believed in them, Holly opened the book back up, finding her page again and setting about putting out the mixing bowls and measuring cups that she would need.

CHAPTER FOUR

Holly looked around her kitchen and grimaced. What a disaster! It looked as if she had been baking for years without cleaning up, instead of only an hour. All she had so far to show for her efforts were a tray of misshapen, charcoaled, hardened lumps. Not at all resembling the hand-sketched drawing that accompanied the recipe in her book. Not willing to admit defeat, Holly scrubbed the kitchen and laid out all of her ingredients and equipment again, determined to make these Holly Cakes work. After all, having now found a Christmas themed treat that shared the same name as her, she could hardly leave it unmade, could she? Donning a fresh apron, Holly started again. As Holly added the first few ingredients to the mixing bowl, two teaspoons of finely grated lemon rind, lime rind, and orange rind, she repeated the words scrawled in the margin of the recipe.

"With the oven hot, the time is right to prime my pot. Lemon, lime, and orange rind,

life's dear friends, all entwined." Holly smiled at the truth of the words, she and

Finn were the same, yet still different enough not to bore each other. Next, she added butter, milk, and vanilla, speaking the words scrawled next to those ingredients in the cookbook. "Milk and butter will charm one another, while vanilla will keep his heart true." It was a nice sentiment. Lastly, she added sugar and chocolate, stirring carefully while she repeated the last remaining words. "Sugar for lips that kiss only you, and chocolate to add spice to all that you do." She smiled slowly, imagining Christmas kisses with her special someone. The batter was looking much more promising than last time, a relief for Holly to see.

She scooped it into a large cavity cupcake tray, placed it in the oven and set the oven timer for twelve minutes.

As Holly waited for the oven timer to go off, she cleaned up the kitchen yet again, thanking her lucky stars that she owned a dishwasher, and didn't have to wash everything herself by hand. At the buzz of the oven timer, Holly donned her oven mitts and opened the oven, carefully lifting the tray of cupcakes out and placing it on a tea towel that she had already laid out on the bench. The cupcakes looked fantastic, perfect little mounds of white perfection, she carefully inserted a skewer into the middle of one of the cupcakes, smiling in delight when she withdrew it and saw small moist crumbs clinging to it, indicating that they were in fact cooked through. Holly left them in the pan to cool for ten minutes, before carefully using a spoon to loosen them around the edges and lifting them out and onto her wire rack to cool completely.

While they cooled, she moved onto the fluffy meringue frosting, placing the egg whites, sugar, and water into a large heatproof bowl, whisking them all to combine. She placed the bowl over a saucepan of simmering water, using an electric hand mixer to beat the egg white mixture for fifteen minutes until stiff peaks formed in the bowl. With the frosting made, and the cupcakes completely cooled, Holly took out her piping bag and piped stunning ribbons of frosting onto one of the cupcakes. She added a slight dusting of Christmas red coloured edible glitter, a smattering of green cachous, and some flecks of gold sprinkles. It looked decadent and Christmassy, and Holly hated to ruin it, but she did anyway, biting into the treat, moaning in delight at the way the flavours exploded on her tongue, at the weightlessness of the mixture, disintegrating on her tongue. It reminded her of Christmas Day on the beach, of summer daydreams, of carefree adventures with friends. It reminded her of Finn, she thought with a start. He would love these. With Finn in mind, Holly set about making another batch, intending to surprise him at work the following day.

When Holly had finally finished for the night, there, in her spotlessly clean kitchen, stood twelve dozen gorgeously decorated Holly Cakes, all proudly waiting to be transported to her bakery in the morning. What started out as a way to settle down, had morphed into making a treat for Finn, and had then somehow taken on a life of its own. Holly had been completely mesmerised with baking these cakes, almost as if she had been in a trance, and had only stopped when she had run out of ingredients. She was exhausted, but thrilled with her efforts, and was keen to see what her customers thought of them tomorrow.

The following day saw Holly wake with a smile, it was December, and after her baking spree last night, the seasonal mojo had returned. She hummed

Christmas carols to herself as she showered and dressed, opting for a knee-length summer dress, with a scooped neckline and a fun Christmas print. She added a pair of glittery red ballet flats, and a slick of red lip gloss, and she was ready to go. Holly all but bounded downstairs, packing her Holly Cakes into the back of her car, and reversing down the driveway. As she turned into the street where her bakery was located, Holly was forced to slam on the brakes, a large crowd of people were milling around. Holly carefully manoeuvred around the crowd and down the alley that ran behind her bakery, leading to her staff only parking lot. As she parked her car, Finn came rushing over, an apologetic look on his face.

"Holly, did you see the crowd?"

"I know, crazy right? Is there some festival or parade or something on that I forgot about?"

"They are here for the bakery Holly; they are waiting for us to open."

"What?!" Holly was so surprised she nearly dropped the box she was holding. "Are you serious? I wonder why?" she mused, passing the box over to Finn. "Cakes," she answered in reply to his raised eyebrow, "a new recipe I'm trying. I'm calling them Holly Cakes."

"Seriously?"

"Too cliched?"

"No, it isn't that, it is just that the first person in the queue told me that they were waiting to buy a Holly Cake. I wasn't aware that you had put anything new on the menu, we usually work on new recipes together."

"Finn," Holly placed her hand on his forearm, stopping him from walking away, "are you being serious right now?" When he didn't answer her, Holly continued.

"I haven't put anything new on the menu, I swear. When I got home yesterday, I was looking through the recipe vault, and I found this old recipe that I thought sounded nice. Honestly, Finn, yesterday was the first time I had ever seen this recipe, let alone attempted to make it. I have no idea if the customers will like it or not. They can't possibly know that I made these last night, they must be talking about something else. In any case," Holly smiled up at Finn, "I actually made these for you, and then I got slightly carried away."

"Exactly how carried away did you get Holly?" Finn's eyes bulged as he saw the sheer number of boxes in the back of Holly's car.

"Twelve dozen." Finn and Holly looked at each other before dissolving into a fit of laughter.

"Well, I'm not sure what the customers are asking for, but let's hope that they like these." Finn smiled, lugging the first box inside.

CHAPTER FIVE

With the Holly Cakes sitting pretty inside her cake cabinet, Holly nodded at Finn to open the doors, a stream of people gushing inside, all talking excitedly, jostling for one of the empty tables and chairs. Within moments all available tables and chairs, both inside the bakery and out on the cute awning-covered patio, were full, and there was still a queue back up the street and around the corner. Holly had never seen anything like it, not on a normal day, certainly closer to Christmas when she stocked her juicy plum puddings, her real rum balls, and her extravagant heavy-laden fruit cakes, they saw crowds of this magnitude. People knew to book in advance or risk missing out, it was rare that Holly had any Christmas treats left after ten o'clock in the mornings during December, being located on a busy shopping street near a school certainly helped.

As Holly was busy serving another customer one of her Holly Cakes, an eerie silence descended on the bakery. Holly paused with her hand in the cake cabinet and looked up, her jaw going slack at the sight that greeted her. At the tables where couples were seated, every single couple who was currently in the bakery enjoying a Holly Cake was holding each other's hands, staring into each other's eyes, unblinking, unspeaking. At the tables where single individuals sat enjoying a Holly Cake, they simply sat there, staring off into space, a relaxed, contented look on their face as they absently munched away. It was uncanny, and a trifle unsettling. The Holly Cake seemed to render people incapable of speech, once the cake had been consumed, talking started up again, quietly, softly. Words are spoken gently, meaningfully. Words spoken with love and kindness. All around her bakery, people were holding hands, whispering words of love.

There were couples embracing as if the passion they felt for each other was too intense for them to wait until they got outside, as if all common sense had abandoned them. Holly had never seen so many people kissing in the same place before, and although she would never admit it to anyone, it made her blush, this open display of affection. Suddenly the bakery erupted into cheers, Holly blinked, wondering what she had missed. There, in the middle of the bakery, a couple embraced, the woman flashing her newly acquired engagement ring. As if spurred on or encouraged by this, another man stood up, kneeling before his partner, declaring his love and asking her to marry him, jumping up to pull her into a hug as she nodded her acceptance. Holly looked towards the kitchen, separate from the bakery shop and café side by a large glass wall, a great talking point, her eyes seeking out Finn. He was already watching her, his gaze intense, boring into hers. Holly felt her chest tighten, warmth flooded her cheeks, and her breath caught. He really was strikingly handsome. If they were such close friends...She let the thought trail off, almost scared of where it would lead, should she allow it to continue.

As Holly sat at her kitchen table later that night, sipping a long, tall glass of lemonade, her eyes fell on the recipe book that she had used last night to create her Holly Cakes. It was just a recipe, wasn't it? The romance that had been in the air at the bakery today was just a fluke, wasn't it? Just part of the romance and the magic of Christmas. The fact that people had queued for her Holly Cakes, without any possible way of knowing that they would be in the bakery today, was just a complete fluke, right? That she had sold all of her Holly Cakes, that all every single customer had wanted to order today had been her Holly Cakes, was just a crazy coincidence, wasn't it? Suddenly Holly wasn't so sure. Giving a nervous laugh, Holly stood, taking her glass of lemonade and heading outside to her grandmother's rose garden. As she wandered around, looking at all of the pretty roses, inhaling their heady scent, Holly was struck with the overwhelming desire to bake gingerbread men.

Holly hadn't baked gingerbread men for years; in fact, she wasn't sure that she had baked them at all since returning from university. Gingerbread houses, yes, by the dozens, all intricately decorated and sold to admiring customers each year for Christmas, but gingerbread men, no. Holly had used to bake gingerbread men every single Christmas with her grandmother growing up, it was their tradition, one that had sadly fallen to the wayside once Holly had started university. They had just never seemed to have any time anymore, and by the time Holly had returned home for Christmas each year, her grandmother had already had everything prepared and waiting, wanting to spoil Holly. After university, Holly had started the bakery and then her grandmother had become ill and Christmas had seemed like such a distant impossibility. Suddenly, baking gingerbread men seemed like the most important thing that Holly would do this Christmas. Turning, she strode back inside, snatching up her newfound recipe book and flipping to the contents page.

Yes! There was a recipe in there for gingerbread, and reading through it quickly, Holly realised that it seemed familiar. It was the same recipe that her grandmother and she had used in the past, her grandmother even had a silly song that they would sing while they baked, Holly remembered fondly, her smile melting away into a questioning frown. Good grief! Holly laughed out loud, her grandmother hadn't been teaching her a song, they had been singing the scribbled margin notes from the recipe book. Amused by the thought that her grandmother might have believed that her ancestors had been witches, Holly decided that for tonight, she would bake her gingerbread men the exact same way her grandmother had taught her, silly songs and all, and if that meant believing that her ancestors had been witches, for one night, then why not, it was Christmas after all, and if there was ever a time for magic to exist, it was now.

As Holly mixed the golden syrup and butter on the stovetop, the smell permeated throughout the kitchen, warming her all the way through to her very soul. She could almost imagine that her grandmother was standing there with her as she sang what she would always know as their silly gingerbread men song.

"The smells I create I use to call; what I want in a man I name it all. I don't care if he's skinny or flat or wide, tall or short, what I want is inside. Sugar for sweetness and ginger for warmth, eggs, butter and flour, will give you your power." She hummed as she rolled out the dough, carefully cutting the gingerbread men out and placing them in the oven to bake. Once ready Holly laid them carefully on her wire rack to cool, smiling at them, falling back into her childhood tradition of naming them. With a start, Holly suddenly remembered that she had always chosen the best one of the lot and named him Finn, her grandmother helping her to carefully wrap him up in cellophane, urging Holly to always remember her choice. Looking over the gingerbread men now, Holly carefully chose the best one, and set it aside, she would take extra care to make sure that one was perfect for Finn.

It was close to midnight by the time that Holly had finally finished decorating her gingerbread man, rows upon rows of handsome little fellows looked back at her, all wearing a variety of hand-piped outfits, three-piece suits, to beachwear, to smart casual outfits, their little faces hand-decorated, even their hairstyles perfectly coiffed. They looked absolutely delightful, and Holly wondered if anybody would actually be able to bring themselves to eat them, or whether they would simply sit on somebody's Christmas table, staring back at them, in pride of place. Finns were the most elaborately decorated of all, Holly spending nearly an hour on him alone. The effort was worth it, gingerbread man Finn now wore a pair of hand-piped loafers complete with shoelaces, denim blue coloured chinos complete with stitching, and a crisp white linen shirt with the sleeves rolled up to his elbow, just as her real-life Finn wore. She had even added his dimple, an extra special touch, as she knew she was one of the very rare people who ever got to see it.

His was the only one that she wrapped in cellophane, reminding herself that this was her choice, that Finn was her choice, just as she knew her grandmother would be urging her to do, had she been here with her.

CHAPTER SIX

When Holly gets to work the following day, there is another queue around the block, this time she doesn't even bother asking Finn what everyone is queuing up for, too scared of what his answer would be. It isn't until she gets closer that she realises that the majority of people who are queuing are men. Not just men, but men that bear a striking resemblance to the gingerbread men that she decorated last night. There were men queueing in three-piece suits, in beachwear, in smart casual outfits, their hair perfectly coiffed.

But it was the sight of Finn, dressed in denim blue coloured chinos, loafers, and a crisp white linen shirt with the sleeves rolled up to his elbow, that nearly caused Holly to run up the curb and into a light pole. He was dressed exactly like the gingerbread man that she had decorated for him last night. How did he know that? Did he, or was it just another stunning coincidence?

Embarrassed at her near car accident, Holly parked as quickly as she could, brushing off Finn's worried questions when he caught up with her, as she was hastily stuffing her gingerbread men into the cabinet ready to sell.

"More baking?" He grinned, happily taking the proffered gingerbread man from Holly. "Oh, my word, this is gorgeous! Thank you, I love how you even dressed him like me, weird though, that this is what I am actually wearing today."

"I know right? Anyway, I couldn't wind down last night, so, yeah," Holly shrugged, "gingerbread men."

"Look," Finn placed an arm on Holly's shoulder, "I know we were super busy yesterday, I'm sorry that we never got to go to the supermarket, I know your seven-day deadline is important to you. When we close today, we'll go straight down, okay?" Holly nodded, having completely forgotten that she had even agreed to go in the first place, so obsessed she had been with her Holly Cakes.

There was definitely something odd going on, Holly decided as she watched people buy her gingerbread men. People seemed to be buying the gingerbread men that looked like them, weirdly so, even down to their shoes. By the time lunch rolled around, Holly was a nervous wreck, convinced that she had somehow evoked magic into her life, that she had somehow managed to not only cast a spell but to actually have it work, twice in as many days. With a break in customers, Holly seized her chance, grabbing Finn by the arm and leading him out to the carpark, where they were unlikely to be overheard.

"Finn, something's wrong." Holly started. "Have you seen how busy the bakery has been these past couple of days, how all everyone wants is what I have just baked, what I baked on a whim, without prior planning?"

"I think it is great Holly, maybe you should try new recipes on a whim more often."

"It isn't the food, Finn," Holly looked around to make sure no one else was there, "I think I cast some kind of summoning spell to get these customers to come here."

Predictably, Finn threw back his head and laughed.

"Finn, please!" Holly heard the desperation in her voice and cringed. "I'm serious. I know you think it sounds like a big joke, but please, just hear me out. The recipe book I found, the one I used to make the Holly Cakes, I think it was a spellbook." Holly ended in a whisper, not wanting the universe to overhear her.

"Holly." Finn stared at her as if she had sprouted a second head, his single word conveying a world of concern.

"No, listen to me. As you mix the batter there is a poem, a song, an enchantment that you need to say, otherwise, the mixture won't turn out, it will become a gloopy mess. Listen, Finn, I know it sounds daft, but I think it was a spell, an actual spell, that worked."

CHAPTER SEVEN

"Okay," Finn nodded, "tell me the spell, tell me what you said."

"With the oven hot, the time is right to prime my pot." Holly blushed at how absurd she sounded, standing out in the middle of the carpark reciting a poem spell to Finn. "Lemon, lime, and orange rind, life's dear friends, all entwined. Milk and butter will charm one another, while vanilla will keep his heart true. Sugar for lips that kiss only you, and chocolate to add spice to all that you do." Finn stared at Holly for the longest time, a peculiar look on his face, causing her to squirm. "Finn?"

"Yes."

"What do you think?"

"I think you are right," he shook his head to clear away the thoughts that crowded there, "something odd is happening, but I am not entirely sure that it is something magical Holly."

"What do you think it is then?"

"I don't know." It was only a small white lie, he couldn't very well tell her the truth now, not until he was certain himself. "Would you like me to look into it for you Holly?"

"Please Finn," she sighed, "I knew I could come to you; I knew you would understand, that I could trust you. Thank you." She reached up, standing on tippy-toe, to kiss his cheek. Finn tried hard not to flinch, not to react, he had become quite good at that over the years, hiding the way that Holly's innocent kisses and touches affected him. Listening to Holly recite that poem, hearing it come from her own sweet lips, had wound his insides up tighter than a watch spring, he felt fit to burst. He dragged his hand through his hair and sighed, he had got to get his emotions under control, before he did or said anything that couldn't be undone or unsaid. Especially now.

Finn watched Holly carefully throughout the rest of the day, surreptitiously so as not to get caught. When only a trickle of customers remained, he tidied up the kitchen, waved goodbye to Holly, and headed out. He wanted to get a start on looking into Holly's poem spell, and he needed to do it without her. If his suspicions were correct, it would not be the news that she was secretly hoping for, and Finn wanted to make sure that his facts were right before he spoke with her, he wanted, no, he needed, to make sure that he had a way of alleviating her disappointment. Finn drove home as quickly as the speed limit would allow, parking in his driveway before crossing the road and letting himself into Holly's house with his key. He went straight to the kitchen, picking up the recipe book from off the kitchen table, and flicking through the pages until he had found the Holly Cake recipe. He read the poem in the margin carefully, yes, he was certain of it now. He knew that this poem had sounded familiar to him somehow, it was the exact same poem that Holly's grandmother had read to him last Christmas, the very same one that she had made him recite back to her.

It was cute for sure, but it definitely was not a spell. Of that Finn was certain, if it had been a spell, then Holly would have been his last Christmas. After all, he had recited it, all the while thinking about Holly, as her grandmother had directed him to once he had admitted that yes, he was in love with her granddaughter. If it had been anything more than a poem, Holly's heart would have been true to Finn, they would have charmed one another, her lips would have kissed only him, but none of that had happened. Not then and not now, because it was not a spell, there obviously had to be a logical explanation for all of the strangeness of the past couple of days. Finn thought back to the conversation that he had had with Holly's grandmother and tried to recall exactly what it was that she had said. She had been sick at the time, the cancer already spreading throughout her body, but she had still been positive, upbeat, not yet aware of just how far the cancer had already spread. She had spoken of Holly and Christmas, and of revamping the bakery for Christmas.

Finn jumped up out of his seat. He remembered. Holly's grandmother had planned to advertise in the local newspaper over the Christmas period, had wanted to try out some old favourite recipes on the customers, to bring in some new seasonal favourites. By the time Christmas had rolled around, Holly's grandmother had been too ill to leave the bed, and Holly had drastically scaled back her hours at the bakery to focus on taking care of her grandmother. Finn had forgotten all about that conversation until just now. He wondered what had happened to the advertising. It couldn't hurt to pop into town and stop off at the newspaper office, you never know, someone might remember. As Finn headed back into town, he passed Holly heading home, waving as he passed. With a bit of luck, he would be able to give Holly an answer soon, some peace of mind, and then everything could go back to being a normal, busy, Christmas season.

The newspaper office was far more helpful than Finn had hoped to imagine. They not only remembered having a conversation with Holly's grandmother last year, but they were also able to pull her original order from their files, handing it over to Finn to read. Finn read through the order with a frown.

"Are you sure that this is the exact one you received? The original order?" He questioned the archives officer.

"Yes sir. I remember thinking that it was odd," the archives officer shrugged, unconcerned, "filing something that had not actually happened yet, but I don't make the rules, I only file."

"Thank you." Finn left the newspaper office, he needed to speak with Holly.

CHAPTER EIGHT

"Finn, hi." Holly opened the door to see Finn on the porch. "I didn't expect to see you tonight."

"Sit with me for a minute?" Finn gestured to the chairs on Holly's front porch.

"Sure." Holly crossed to the two-person swing, sitting, patting the seat next to her for Finn to join her, which he did.

"Holly, I found out something about the bakery today, about your wonderful recipes, and about your grandmother." He took her hand in his. "When you told me the poem earlier today, it sounded familiar to me somehow, and I was right Holy, I had heard it before, your grandmother had told it to me last Christmas, she had made me recite it actually." Finn smiled at the memory. "I'm sorry, I didn't remember until today, otherwise I would have told you earlier. Your grandmother also told me something else, she had wanted to put an ad in the local newspaper last year, she had wanted to introduce some of her old Christmas favourites onto the menu, as a surprise, for you."

"Let me guess," Holly whispered, her throat tight, "gingerbread men and Holly Cakes?"

"Yes," Finn confirmed. "The only thing is Holly, for whatever reason, the ad had been archived by the newspaper, they had misread the writing, they had thought that it was meant to be placed this year, not last."

"That's how everyone knew to come into the bakery?"

"Yes."

"I knew that it wasn't magic, I'm not stupid Finn." Holly defended.

"I never thought you were," Finn confirmed.

"It was just a silly little poem, a ridiculous song to try and keep a little girl entertained and interested in baking, that was all it ever was."

Holly was disappointed, achingly so. She knew it wasn't magic, she knew that, but still, a part of her had hoped that the reason would be a tiny bit mysterious, instead of simply an error. That was it, Holly was done with magic, and maybe spells, and chanting poems while she baked. From now on, she would be professional, a proper baker, here at home and at work. Finn didn't linger, he knew that Holly would need time to process everything that he had told her, everything that he had discovered. He kissed her cheek goodnight, and left her on the porch swing, deep in thought.

Holly had not slept well last night, after Finn had left, she had wandered through her house, pausing to look at all the old photographs of her and her grandmother that hung on the walls. She missed her grandmother. This would be the first Christmas that Holly had without her grandmother and she wasn't entirely sure she would get through it. Well, she knew the logistics of the day, she would spend it with Finn and his family, like she had every year for as long as she could remember. This year though, her grandmother would be missing, and she would be missed. Finding out the truth about the bakery, about her new recipes, about the mix up with the advertising, had all compounded Holly's grief, and she had lain awake last night, staring up at the ceiling, wishing with all of her might that she could have had just one more moment with her grandmother, just one more hug, one more conversation. She had eventually cried herself to sleep sometime after midnight.

Holly's alarm blared at her far too early, and she dragged herself from bed, not at all inspired by the thought of going into work. Once again there was a queue outside of her bakery, lined up around the corner, which should have made Holly happy, but only served to make her feel deflated. She hadn't believed in witches to start with, yet when she had thought that she had somehow conjured up a magical spell to befall her bakery, the crowds had been exciting, and now, they were just Christmas shoppers. The irony was not lost on Holly. The day dragged by for Holly, she served customers, she cleared tables, and she spoke with Finn, all of these things she did on autopilot, automatically and without any conscious thought. She saw the worried looks Finn shot her way but couldn't bring herself to do anything about it. She was tired, deflated, defeated.

Holly was glad to finally close the bakery and get back home. She changed into some gardening clothes, and took her shears out into the front yard, attacking the overgrown bougainvillaea with fervour. An hour later, covered in sweat and small scratches from the bougainvillaea thorns, Holly threw down her shears in defeat, heading for the shade of her patio, passing the letterbox on the way, surprised to see a stack of letters waiting for her. One, in particular, caught her eye, a large, heavy, linen envelope, bearing the name and logo of a prestigious law firm located in town. Slipping her fingernail under the flap, she slit the envelope open, pulling out a letter, along with a second, smaller, envelope. The letter is brief, and straight to the point. The law firm was retained by her grandmother, to create and execute her will. They had been instructed to send this letter on to Holly, from her grandmother, at the beginning of

December. The letter finished by telling Holly that if she had any questions, she should feel free to give them a call, and they would be happy to help her.

Holly pulled the second letter out of the smaller envelope, her hands shaking slightly at the all too familiar script, her grandmother's handwriting. With tears running down her cheeks, she read her grandmother's last letter to her.

Dear Holly,

If you are reading this it means that you are celebrating your first Christmas without me, and I do hope that you are celebrating Holly, you adore Christmas, you are just like me in that respect. I know that you will miss me, but don't let that cause you to miss out on everything else. Christmas is full of magic Holly; it is the most magical time of the year. Don't give up on that magic, remember that magic, and love, are in the small things, and they are all around us, if only we open our eyes to really see. Follow your heart. I love you darling girl, and I am so proud of you.

Gran

CHAPTER NINE

After reading her grandmother's letter last night, Holly had done some serious thinking, about her life, about her future, about what it was, and who it was, that she really wanted. It was funny to think that it would take her grandmother's death, and a letter from the grave, to make Holly see what she had known all along. She wanted to race across to Finn, to tell him what she had discovered, but she held herself in check, suddenly shy. What if Finn didn't want to hear about Holly's discovery? What if he thought that it was a crazy idea? So, Holly held her tongue, choosing to stay home instead, pottering around the house, tidying up a little bit, and pulling the Christmas ornaments and tree down from the attic. She would put it up tomorrow, really make her house Christmassy. With that plan in place, it was a happy Holly that went to bed, and a contented Holly that slept soundly, for the first time in a long while.

Pulling up to work the following day, Holly found herself smiling at the large queue of people waiting to get inside the bakery. These lovely people, her wonderful customers, were one of the reasons that she loved running her bakery so much, they gave her day meaning. She wasn't just selling them a loaf of bread or a decorated cake, she was selling them a memory, a slice of family. Holly was still smiling as she let herself in the back door, coming to a sudden stop when her eyes met with complete darkness, instead of the brightly lit bakery that she was expecting.

"Finn? Are you here?" She called out, surely, he was here, he was never late.

"Wait right there, I'm coming to get you."

"Okay," Holly called back, intrigued. She saw a light flickering, and then Finn appeared by her side, a large grin on his face.

"Morning Holly, you look nice today." He winked at her, causing her insides to flutter. "Follow me."

Holly followed Finn through to the dark interior of the bakery, stopping once they reached the middle of the bakery floor.

"Are you ready?" Finn asked.

"Yes," Holly whispered, excitement coursing through her veins.

"Happy Christmas Holly." The bakery was suddenly lit with hundreds of strands of fairy lights, all sparkling and twinkling at her. Holly gasped in delight, it was like her own private winter wonderland, a magical secret Christmas cave. There, in the middle of the room, stood a table with a single gingerbread house on top of it. Holly walked over to the table, struck by the intricate craftsmanship of the gingerbread house. The gingerbread house was a perfect replica of her bakery, it even had little windows, tables and chairs on the patio, and a frilly awning. In front of the bakery stood a little gingerbread man, a little gingerbread woman, two little gingerbread children, and one little gingerbread dog. The gingerbread woman bore a striking resemblance to Holly. Altogether, it was absolute perfection, and it left Holly speechless.

"Finn." Holly was dumbfounded, mouth gaping open as she slowly twirled the cake stand around, trying to take everything in. "Did you do all of this?"

"Yes. I did it for you." When Holly didn't respond, Finn spoke again. "It is a family Holly, for you, your Christmas wish."

"Oh, Finn, it's gorgeous, it really is, but I already have a family." Holly stepped closer to Finn, inhaling a deep breath, deciding to be brave. "I have you." She whispered. "You are all I have ever wanted, all I have ever needed Finn, I'm sorry it took me so long to see it."

"Holly," there was wonder in Finn's voice, "do you really mean that?"

"You are my choice, Finn; you always have been." Holly looked deeply into Finn's eyes, smiling, all of her fears dissipating when she saw his love reflected back at her.

"Holly, I love you, and I have been in love with you for years. Your grandmother knew, that is why she made me recite that poem." Finn smiled down at Holly. "I'm sorry that I was too scared to tell you how I really felt, I was so worried about losing you, about losing our friendship, that I kept quiet." He gripped her hands in his. "Do you know what my surname means Holly?"

"Teleios? No."

"It is Greek for perfect. So, you see Holly, you really did get your Mr Perfect."

"I did, and I intend to keep him, for always and forever." Holly reached up to wrap her arms around Finn's neck, pulling his head down to meet hers.

As Finn's lips met hers, in a kiss that was full of promise and love, Holly decided that her grandmother was right, there is magic and love everywhere, you just need to know where to look.

THE END

BONUS RECIPES

HOLLY CAKES

Two teaspoons of finely grated lemon rind
Two teaspoons of finely grated lime rind
Two teaspoons of finely grated orange rind
350g butter, chopped
180g white chocolate, chopped
2 cups caster sugar
2 teaspoons vanilla extract
1 ½ cups milk
3 large eggs
2 cups plain flour
¾ cup self-raising flour

Preheat the oven to 160 degrees Celsius.
Combine lemon, lime, orange rind, butter, chocolate, sugar, vanilla, and milk in a saucepan over low heat. Stir until smooth.
Pour into a large bowl. Allow to cool for 10 minutes. Add eggs. Stir to combine. Add plain and self-raising flours. Stir to combine.
Scoop into a large cavity muffin or cupcake tray. Bake until a skewer inserted into the middle has moist crumbs clinging to it.
Stand in cake pan for 10 minutes. Cool on a wire rack.

To make the fluffy meringue frosting...

4 egg whites
2 cups caster sugar
¼ cup cold water

Place egg whites, sugar, and water in large heatproof bowl. Whisk to combine.
Place bowl over a saucepan of simmering water. Using an electric hand mixer, beat egg white mixture for 15 minutes or until stiff peaks form.

GINGERBREAD MEN

Two teaspoons of ground cinnamon
Two teaspoons of ground ginger
½ teaspoon of bicarbonate of soda
75g butter, chopped
2 large eggs
3 cups plain flour
¾ cup golden syrup
¾ cup self-raising flour
¾ firmly packed brown sugar

Preheat the oven to 180 degrees Celsius.
Place the butter, sugar, and syrup in saucepan over low heat. Cook, stirring, for 10 minutes. Remove from heat.
Pour into a large bowl. Allow to cool for 20 minutes.
Sift flours, bi carbonate of soda, ginger, and cinnamon together. Add eggs to butter mixture, stir until just combined. Add flours mixture. Stir until combined and mixture forms a dough.
Knead on a lightly floured surface. Shape into two discs. Cover with plastic wrap. Refrigerate for an hour.
Line baking trays with baking paper. Roll dough out. Cut out gingerbread men or other shapes from dough.
Bake for 12 minutes. Cool on trays.

To make the royal icing...

2 egg whites
3 cups pure icing sugar
1 tablespoon lemon juice
Food colouring, optional

Whisk egg white in a bowl until frothy. Gradually add icing sugar. Whisk until smooth. Stir in lemon juice. Colour as required. Use icing placed inside a piping bag to 'dress' your gingerbread men.

About The Author

An international bestselling and award-winning author of sweet contemporary romance, Kathleen's novels showcase thought-provoking plots and strong emotions that have been likened to a Hallmark movie. Featuring feisty heroines and strong heroes, where everyone gets a happily ever after. To discover more about Kathleen: https://linktr.ee/KathleenRyder